Peppa Pig

and the
Muddy Puddles

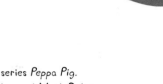

First paperback edition 2014

Library of Congress Catalog Card Number 2012942611
ISBN 978-0-7636-6523-4 (hardcover)
ISBN 978-0-7636-7226-3 (paperback)

15 16 17 18 SCP 10 9 8 7 6

Printed in Humen, Dongguan, China

This book was typeset in Peppa.
The illustrations were created digitally.

Candlewick Entertainment
An imprint of Candlewick Press
99 Dover Street
Somerville, Massachusetts 02144

visit us at www.candlewick.com

Peppa Pig and the Muddy Puddles

CANDLEWICK
ENTERTAINMENT

Mummy Pig and Daddy Pig are tucking Peppa and George into bed.

"There's so much rain!" Peppa says.
"That means there will be muddy puddles to jump in tomorrow,"
Mummy Pig says with a smile.

The *splish-splash-splosh* of raindrops on the window sings Peppa and George to sleep. They dream of muddy puddles.

It rains . . .

and rains . . .

and rains.

The next morning, the sun is shining.
Daddy Pig runs out to jump in a muddy puddle.
But he lands in a big pool of water instead!

"Oh! How did this water get here?" Daddy Pig asks.

"And where are the muddy puddles?" asks Peppa.

Quack!
Quack!
Quack!

Splash!

"Our house is on an island!"
says Peppa.

"Oh, dear," says Mummy Pig.
"What will we do?"

Granny Pig and Grandpa Pig arrive on their boat.
"Ahoy, there!" Grandpa Pig says. "Wonderful boating weather!"

"We're going to the store," says Granny Pig.

"Can George and I come, too?" asks Peppa.

"Yes! We'll do the shopping for everybody!"

Squawk!

"Polly can remember our shopping list.
She's very good at that,"
Granny Pig says.
"Who's a clever parrot?"

"SQUAWK!
Who's a clever parrot?"
says Polly.
Polly is very good at
repeating what people say.

Peppa, George, Grandpa Pig, Granny Pig, and Polly motor across the water. It's fun, but there are no muddy puddles.

Each house is on its own island.

They go from house to house, asking everyone what they need from the store.

Suzy Sheep
asks for chocolate.

"SQUAWK! Chocolate!" Polly repeats.

Granddad Dog needs a newspaper,
and Danny Dog wants a comic book.

"SQUAWK! Newspaper!
Comic book!" Polly repeats.

Grampy Rabbit wants cheese.

"SQUAWK! Cheese!"
Polly repeats.

Grandpa Pig's boat arrives at the supermarket.

"Hello!" says Miss Rabbit. "What can I get you?"

"Polly knows!" Peppa says proudly.

Squawk!

Polly opens her beak.
"Who's a clever parrot?
Who's a clever parrot?" she says.
Polly has forgotten the list!

"Don't worry," says Peppa. "I remember. . . ."

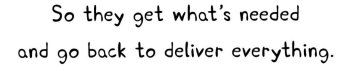

So they get what's needed
and go back to deliver everything.

"Cheese," says Grampy Rabbit.
"Thank you!"

"A newspaper
and comic book,"
say Granddad Dog and Danny Dog.
"Thank you!"

"Chocolate!" says Suzy Sheep. "Thank you!"

"Chocolate for dinner?" asks Mummy Sheep.

Peppa and George are very sleepy when they arrive back home.

"Did you have fun?" asks Mummy Pig.

"Yes," says Peppa. "We got lots of things at the store.
We got something for everyone."

Snort!

But Peppa is sad.

She didn't get what *she* wanted.

There were no muddy puddles at all.

The next morning,
the sun is shining brightly
in the clear blue sky.
Polly Parrot comes to visit.

Grandpa Pig's boat is stuck
on Peppa's front lawn!

"Oh!" Granny Pig says,
looking out from the boat.
"The flood is over!"

They all look around.

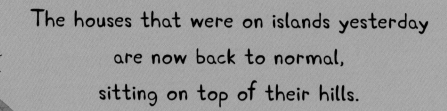

The houses that were on islands yesterday
are now back to normal,
sitting on top of their hills.

The water that Peppa
and George boated in
is gone.

And at the bottom
of their very own hill they see . . .

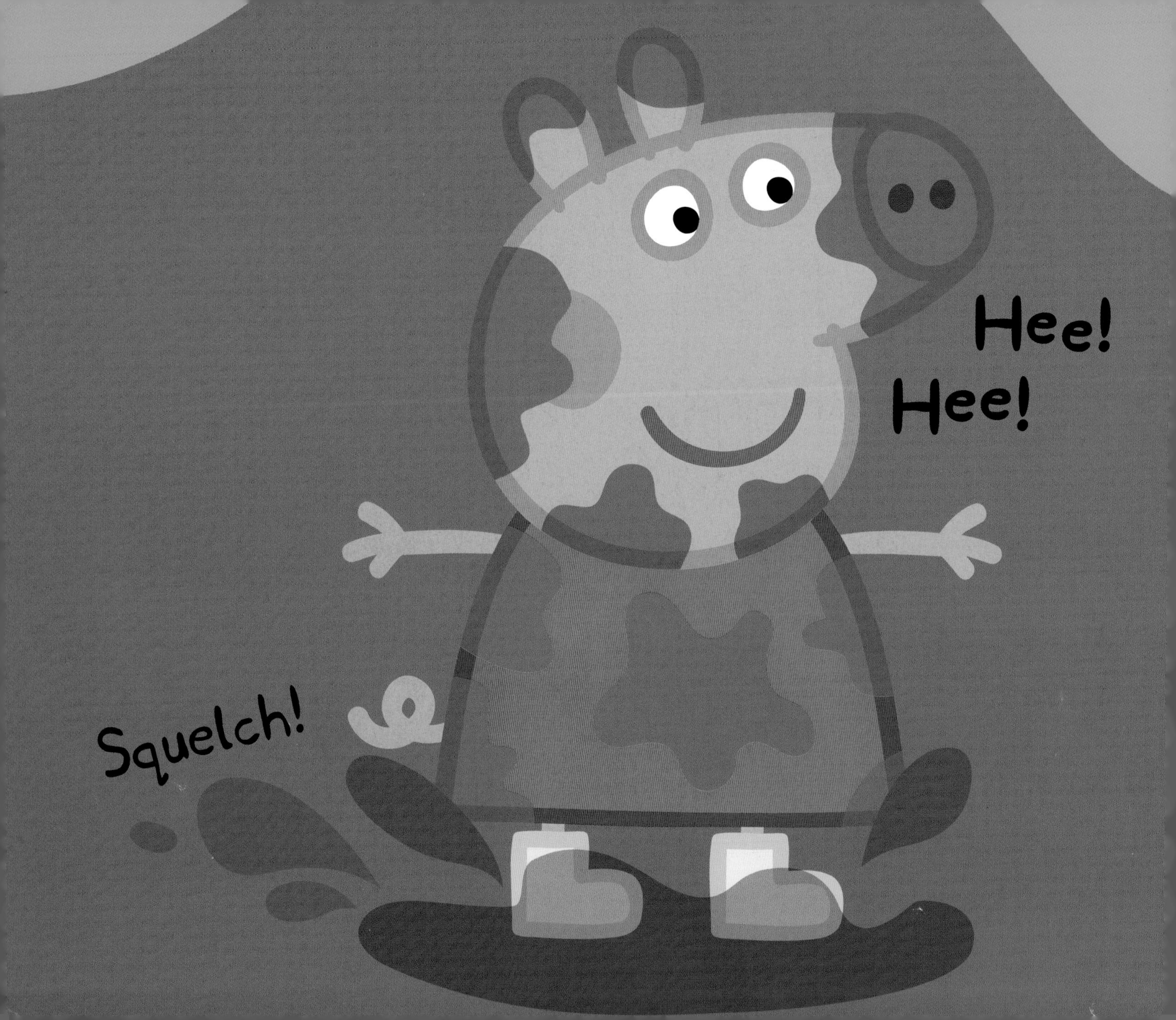
Hee!
Hee!
Squelch!

a great big

muddy puddle . . .

Hee!
Hee!

Squelch!

big enough
for everyone!